HOW LOW COULD WE GO?

"Listen up," Zo whispered. "These boys are trying to push us around."

"Zo," I said, "we can't fall into their trap. We should pass the ball and find the open man—"

"Pat!" Zo interrupted. "I know we want to play a good game, but this isn't just about hoops. It's about attitude. These boys think they're the bad boys of Thompsonville, so we gotta be the baddest on the yard, you know what I'm sayin'?"

"For once, Zo's right," Cheryl agreed. "Let's play with some attitude. Come on, now!"

"All right." I finally decided. "We can't let these boys push us around. Let's get tough."

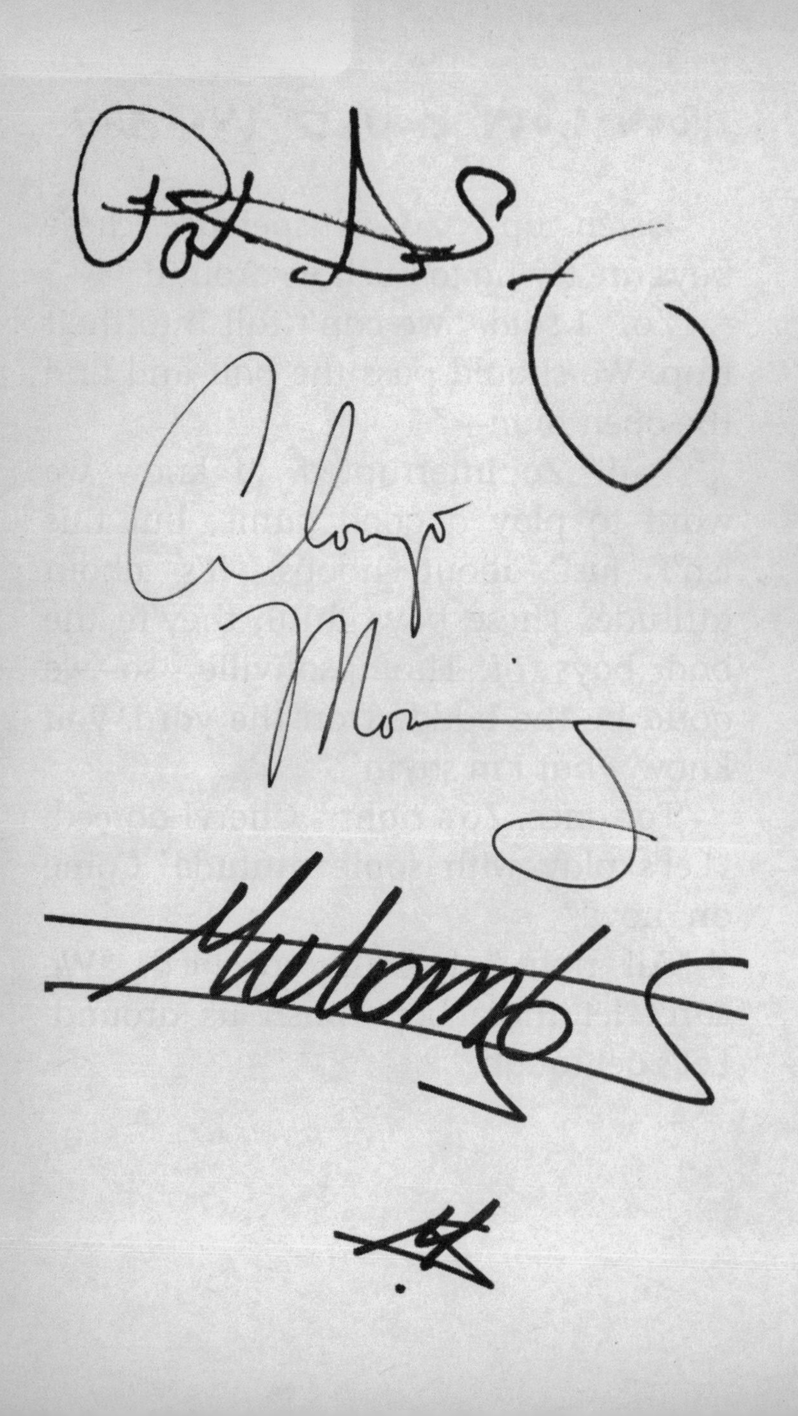

IN YOUR FACE!

Robb Armstrong
Illustrated by Bruce Smith

A Division of
HarperCollins*Publishers*

In Your Face!

Produced by:
17th Street Productions
33 West 17th Street
New York, NY 10011

ISBN: 0-06-107068-8
Library of Congress Catalog Card Number: 98-70305

Printed in the United States of America
First Edition, 1998

Patrick's Pals *is dedicated to my children,*
Patrick, Jr., Randi, and Corey, and
in loving memory of my mother,
Dorothy

The artist gratefully acknowledges the assistance of Kenny Thompkins in preparing the interior illustrations for this book.

Chapter 1

The Bad Boys of Thompsonville

"Yo, fellas! Check out MC Beanpole over here! Ha-*haaaa*!"

The loudmouthed cackle took me by surprise and tripped me up in the middle of a sweet move to the hoop. The brick went flying out of my hands and I fell facedown on the hot asphalt. Who was that nasty dude calling me names? He had a posse with him, and they cracked up as I let out a groan.

It was one of those scorching

hot summer Sundays at Douglass Park, and I'd been shooting hoops like usual with my team, the Bulldogs. We were having a great practice until Cackling Boy and his crew interrupted us.

"Nice move, Beanpole!" the boy shouted with another big laugh.

From my place on the ground, I looked up at the five guys behind him, who were howling with laughter.

My blood started boiling. I'd never seen this crew before in my life and they were clowning me in front of my teammates!

My boys Alonzo "Zo" Mourning and Dikembe Mutombo ran over and helped me up. Cheryl Hillman—the only girl on our team—and "Fat Craig" Adams checked to see if I was all right.

But my best friend, Ronnie Miller, hung back. He was keeping his distance. I thought he was a little scared of these kids, whoever they were. And I'll admit, they were pretty scary. The Cackling Crew couldn't have been more than thirteen years old, but they looked like they were in high school. And they must have been taking their ugly pills every day, because they were the biggest goon squad I'd ever seen in Thompsonville.

"Awww," said the boy who wouldn't stop messing with me. "Does Beanpole need some help getting up? I guess he's too skinny to stand up by himself."

I shook Zo and Dikembe off me and stepped to the nasty dude.

"Do I know you?" I demanded, looking him in the eye with a cold hard stare.

"Nah, you don't know me, boy," he said. "The name's Carlos." He held out his arms like he thought he was famous or something. "And this here's my team . . . the Warriors. Warriors in the haaaouse!"

"*Boo-yaa!*" shouted the Warriors.

Carlos was the biggest and the ugliest of the bunch. He had picked up my ball and he was palming it with one hand. His head was covered with nappy dreds and he looked like he could break some ninja blocks with his chin.

But I wasn't scared of him.

"Yo, Carlos," said my boy Zo as he stepped toward Carlos. Zo jabbed a pointy finger up at him and said angrily, "You better *recognize!*"

Zo was totally in Carlos's face. Well, actually, he was more like in his chest. But he was looking up at his face.

"Excuse me, baby boy?" Carlos

shouted down at Zo. I don't think Carlos could even believe little Zo would try to challenge him. But that was because he didn't know Zo.

See, Zo's the youngest member of the Bulldogs and he's my good friend. But the boy is C-R-A-Z-Y! He's just an eight-year-old kid, and small for his age, but he thinks he's seven feet tall and in the NBA. He talks more trash than the local dump. Someday he's going to get in trouble.

"I'll handle this," I said calmly, pushing Zo back behind me.

"Carlos," I said. "Are you trying to set something off, or what?"

"Well, I don't see any other beanpoles around here," he smirked, swinging his nappy dreds all over the place. "Fellas? Y'all see any other beanpoles trippin' around on the court?"

His goon squad replied with a chorus of "Uh-uh"s and "Nope"s, and started howling with laughter again.

I felt like I was going to pop. I was clenching my teeth so hard, my jaw was starting to ache.

The rest of my teammates were about to lose their cool, too, I could tell. They kept creeping closer and closer to Carlos and me. Dikembe had a nasty scowl on his face, and Fat Craig and Cheryl were both letting out little angry grunts.

But I checked myself, and chilled.

After all, it's not like this was the first time anyone had called me "Beanpole." When you're twelve years old and you're already almost six feet, someone's going to call you Beanpole; it's not exactly an original insult. But even though I'm tall and a little on the skinny side, I'm still strong.

"My name's Patrick," I told Carlos. "Patrick Ewing, not Beanpole. And that's my ball."

I unclenched my fist and put my hand out for the rock.

"What's that you said?" Carlos pulled the ball away. He cupped his hand to his ear and got all up in my face. *"Patricia?* Did you say your name was Patricia?"

Even though I believe violence never really solves anything, I was just about ready to punch this guy's lights out.

"We all were just wonderin', Patricia," Carlos giggled, "do you want to be a cheerleader for the Warriors?"

"Are you just gonna take that, Patrick?" Zo squeaked, trying to peek his head up over my shoulder.

"Yeah, Patrick," Cheryl said from behind me. "He can't talk to you like that. Give him a piece of your mind."

Cheryl had some serious game and some serious attitude to match. If Cheryl had something on her mind, it quickly found its way to her mouth. And then Fat Craig was going to repeat whatever she said.

"Yeah, Patrick," Fat Craig called out over my other shoulder. "Tell him what time it is!"

"Stay out of it," I said, pushing the

rest of the Bulldogs a little farther back.

"Yo, Patrick," Ronnie whispered. He was standing way behind the rest of the Bulldogs. It was the first time he'd opened his mouth since the Warriors had showed up, and he sounded pretty shaky.

"Not now, Ronnie!" I said.

I turned back to Carlos.

"Look, Carlos," I said with my biggest smile, "I'm not looking to mix it up with you, know what I'm sayin'? So why don't you just give me the ball back and we'll—"

Suddenly, Ronnie's hand grabbed my jersey and jerked me away from Carlos. Ronnie's green eyes were bulging out of his head and he was shaking his wiry arm in my face. Something was wrong. He was trying to shut me up.

And he looked very scared.

THE CHALLENGE

CHAPTER 2

Ronnie yanked me away from Carlos and we formed a quick huddle with the rest of the Bulldogs.

"I've heard of this crew, man," Ronnie whispered. He looked like he was telling a ghost story, he was so scared. "Yo, these are the bad boys of Thompsonville, man. They play over at Wilkins Park and they play rough, Pat. Don't mess with them!"

"These chumps?" Zo squeaked, running his crazy eight-year-old mouth again. "These boys are chump change! I could house them with one leg."

"Nah, this is for real, Zo," Ronnie whispered. "They're just bad news."

"Quit lyin'!" Cheryl scolded, hitting Ronnie on the shoulder.

"Yeah, stop lyin'!" Fat Craig agreed.

Fat Craig always figured Cheryl knew what she was talking about.

"Straight up!" said Ronnie. "We should all break out of here right now before something jumps off."

"No—" Dikembe started. But that was all he got to say, because big bad Carlos crashed in on our huddle.

"Uh, excuse me, ladies?" Carlos grinned as he shoved Fat Craig aside.

Ronnie jumped back about three feet. I'd seen him nervous before, but I'd never seen him this nervous.

"See," Carlos said, baring his crooked teeth, "we've beaten every team we played, so we're down here looking for some competition." Carlos stood with his arms crossed, as the other Warriors gathered behind him. "Any of you *scrubs* know where we can find some real players to get a game on?"

Zo jumped at Carlos. "Who are you callin' a scrub, *chump*?" Zo shouted up Carlos's nose.

"Who you callin' a chump, *baby?*" Carlos shouted as he bent down to get in Zo's mug.

"Who you callin' a baby, *chump?*" Zo belted back at Carlos.

Zo was about to get himself smacked, so I stepped between them to break it up.

"That's enough," I said firmly, pushing Zo and Carlos away from each other. I pointed at Zo. "Chill."

Carlos grinned and spat on the ground.

"Yes!" my boy Dikembe yelled as he stepped in front of me and Zo. He looked right at Carlos. "You should be chilled. You should not be disrespecting my possum!"

The Warriors started laughing big time.

"*Posse*, Dikembe," I whispered, trying to help him out. "Disrespecting your posse."

Dikembe's my boy. He's the tallest member of the Bulldogs, and he's got mad knowledge. I mean, he speaks like nine languages or something. But he just came to this country from Zaire in Africa, and even though he speaks great English, he hasn't exactly gotten the slang down yet.

"You hear that, fellas?" Carlos screamed, doubled over with laughter. His whole ugly crew was practically falling down laughing at Dikembe. "Shaka Zulu here says we're disrespecting his *possum!*"

But Dikembe didn't back down for a second.

"Shaka Zulu was a great warrior," Dikembe said, with his hand on Zo's shoulder, kind of protecting him. "You should be ashamed to call yourselves warriors."

That shut the Warriors up. There was full silence for about five seconds.

"Is that a challenge, Shaka Zulu?" asked Carlos. "Are you trying to mess with Carlos?" he sneered, getting up in Dikembe's face. "Nobody messes with me . . . because I'm *the man,*" Carlos went on.

Cheryl walked up to Carlos and put her hands on her hips. She looked up at him with her toughest frown.

"Are we supposed to be scared?" Cheryl asked. "'Cause the Bulldogs ain't sweating you and your funky-looking team. We'd love to school you in the game of basketball."

A vein started bulging out of Carlos's neck. I thought he was going to hit her. But he stopped himself short and just grinned.

"Y'all are the saddest-looking bunch of scrubs I've ever seen," Carlos said. "The Warriors would grind your little crew into hamburger in about five minutes."

"Prove it!" Fat Craig jumped up next to Cheryl.

"Is that a challenge, fat boy?" said Carlos, almost laughing as he looked back at his crew.

"You got it, baby!" Zo screamed

fiercely, getting up in Carlos's face again. "Anytime. Anywhere. We'll shake and bake you. We'll quake you."

"Zo! Stop trippin'," Ronnie begged.

"Nah!" Zo shrieked. "We ain't backin' down. Right here. Right now. Bulldogs versus Warriors. Douglass Park is our court. I say let's get busy!"

"I'm down with that," said Cheryl, sliding her head from side to side.

"I'm downer than down," said Fat Craig, sliding his big butt from side to side.

"Well, what do *you* say, Patricia?" Carlos asked, getting up in my face again. "You ready to get dunked on?"

Now, like I said, I don't think fists are the way to settle an argument. But hoops can be a really good way to settle a score.

"What do I say?" I said, looking at Carlos. "It's on!"

CHAPTER 3

Too Much Talkin'

"Check me out!" Zo shouted as he dribbled between his legs.

Zo was running his mouth and showing off. And it was not making the Warriors happy.

"Watch me work, boy," Zo boasted right in the face of the Warrior trying to defend him. "'Cause you know one thing I always could do . . . was finger roll!"

Zo busted a quick stutter step, drove right, and flipped the ball to the hoop.

Swish!

"*Awwww*. It's all good," Zo announced as he floated around the court like a butterfly with a giant grin on his face.

FINGER ROLL!

I flashed Zo a hard look. All that trash-talking was making the Warriors angry.

"I ain't even tryin' to hear that, baby boy!" Carlos yelled. "Yo, just get me the ball!" he screamed to his teammates.

The sun beat down on us hard. I swear you could have cooked up some eggs and bacon on the asphalt.

Carlos took the ball at the top of the key. Just our luck, Ronnie was covering him. Ronnie is about the worst basketball player in Thompsonville.

"This is for you, Junior!" Carlos shouted.

He faked left, pounded the rock on the

court and took off. Ronnie ducked like a bomb was about to hit. And it did.

"*Boo-yaa!*" Carlos belted as he slammed the rock through the hoop, grabbing the rim like a pull-up bar and swinging on it extra long before he came down.

"Why don't you mop up my sweat, Youngster?" Carlos taunted.

"Just get me the ball, Pat," Zo said.

"No, Zo," I insisted, taking Zo by the shoulders, trying to calm him down. "Stay cool. Just play the game."

"Yeah, yeah, okay, Pat," Zo muttered. But the second he got the ball . . . "I got *skiiills*! They're multiplying! And I'm losing control. Try and catch me, baby. I got my groove on. I'm the one you can't stand when the ball's in my hand."

"Get up on him, D-Rock!" Carlos yelled to the brother covering Zo. "Shut that baby boy up."

D-Rock got in even closer on Zo. He was towering over Zo with his long pumped-up arms and his big square

head. It looked like Zo was being guarded by Frankenstein.

But Zo didn't seem to notice. He was in his own trash-talking zone. "Get ready," Zo taunted D-Rock. "Here's some drama that might upset your mama."

Zo put the ball on the floor for another move, but D-Rock hip-checked Zo flat! Zo's hands slapped down on the asphalt

and the ball rolled onto the court.

One of the Warriors scooped it up,

dribbled upcourt three times, and hoisted up a quick shot.

Swish!

"Yeeah!" The Warriors all patted each other on the back.

"Nice steal, D-Rock," said Carlos.

"Steal?" Dikembe shouted in disbelief. "That was a foul! That call smells very bad."

"I don't know, Shaka Zulu," Carlos said. "I thought that bad smell was you."

The Warriors laughed.

But Dikembe was right; the call stank. D-Rock had intentionally slammed into Zo. The Warriors were playing dirty.

"Time out!" Zo screamed as he picked himself up and brushed himself off.

Zo ran around the court, grabbing each of the Bulldogs by their jerseys and pulling us into a huddle.

"Listen up," Zo whispered. "These boys are trying to push us around."

"Zo," I said, "we can't fall into their

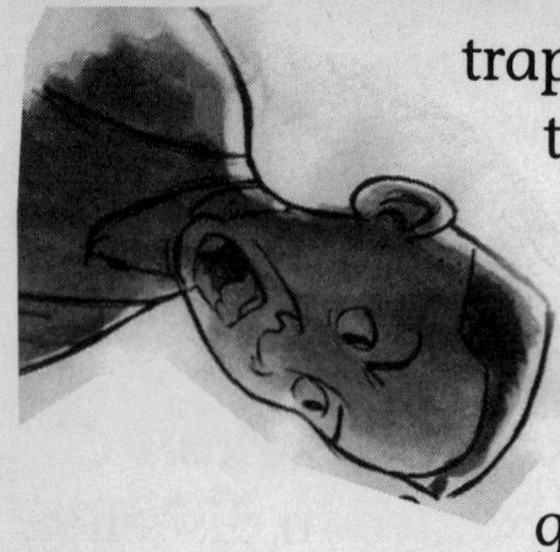

trap. We should pass the ball and find the open man—"

"Pat!" Zo interrupted. "I know we want to play a good game, but this isn't just about hoops. It's about attitude. These boys think they're the bad boys of Thompsonville, so we gotta be the baddest on the yard, you know what I'm sayin'?"

"For once, Zo's right," Cheryl agreed. "Get me the ball and I'll show the Warriors who's the toughest team in Douglass Park. Bulldogs!"

"Bulldogs!" Fat Craig yelled, slapping five with Cheryl. "Let's bully them right back, yo."

Now, I didn't want to play a dirty game. That's not my style. But my teammates did have a point about standing up to the Warriors and putting them in their place.

"Pat," Zo went on, "you just gonna let these boys call you Patricia, and mess with Dikembe? That ain't right. We gotta get tough!"

"I agree with them," Dikembe said. "These boys are not giving us preps."

"Props," I corrected. Dikembe gave me a big goofy grin.

"That's what I said," he joked. "Props."

"Pat," said Cheryl. "Let's play with some attitude. Come on, now!"

Cheryl put her hand out in the center of the huddle. Zo put his hand on top of hers. Dikembe and Fat Craig threw their hands in. They looked at me, expectantly.

"All right," I finally decided. "We can't let these boys just push us around. Let's get tough."

I threw my hand in with my teammates'.

"Yeah!" the team agreed. Except Ronnie, who was busy chewing on his fingernails.

"Ronnie, come on," said Cheryl, sounding like she was his mom telling him to clean his room. We were all waiting for Ronnie to throw his hand in.

"Look, you guys," Ronnie said, "this has to be a clean game, because if we let the Warriors get out of hand—"

"Ronnie, are you down with the Bulldogs or not?" Zo demanded.

Ronnie looked over to me and I quickly nodded my head to let him know we could handle them.

Ronnie frowned, but he laid his hand down on top of the rest of ours.

"One, two, three. Go, Bulldogs!" we all shouted as we came out of the huddle, growling like dogs.

Chapter 4

Copping a 'Tude

"Rebound, Elroy!" Carlos screamed at one of his teammates. "Quick! Grab the rock!"

Ronnie and Elroy were battling for position to snatch a rebound. Even though Ronnie was the taller of the two players, he looked like a carrot stick next to Mile-Wide Elroy.

Elroy was actually the shortest player on the Warriors. He was also the *widest* player on the Warriors.

Everything about him was too wide. His shoulders were a mile apart. So were his eyes. And his nose looked like a two-car garage.

Ronnie threw his hands up for the rebound, and Elroy rammed him to the ground to grab the ball!

"Why don't you take yourself out of the game, chump?" Elroy shouted down at Ronnie. "You better check yourself before you wreck yourself!"

Ronnie looked at me and raised his eyebrows, but he didn't say anything. He just got up and back into the game.

Fat Craig grabbed the rebound, but one of the Warriors managed to steal it. He passed the ball back out to that scary Frankenstein-looking D-Rock.

Zo got right up on him, even though his head came only to D-Rock's chest. Zo was looking for payback.

Just as D-Rock went into his move, Zo slapped the ball right out of his hands. Then Zo butted his head right into D-Rock's gut!

"*Ooompf!*" D-Rock grunted as the wind was knocked out of him.

"Oops," said Zo, dribbling and looking down at D-Rock. "That's what you call a steal back in Chump City, right?"

I couldn't believe what Zo had just done,

but Cheryl and Fat Craig let out a big laugh.

"Zo! Zo! Check it, I'm open!" Cheryl was waving her hands like crazy.

Zo passed the rock to Cheryl, who went into a mad dribbling display and then took off for the hoop. Just as her defender was about to catch up with her, Dikembe stepped out and set a cold hard pick.

"*Ugh,*" groaned the poor Warrior as he bounced off Mount Mutombo.

Cheryl took the clear lane and laid it in. Point.

"That was for disrespecting my . . . posse!" Dikembe shouted.

"Dikembe!" I yelled, and gave him a hard look. "Stay cool, man." He shrugged, looking embarrassed.

But the game just kept getting uglier and uglier. Everyone was talking trash, and elbows were flying left and right. The hot sun was killing us all. I was getting a monster headache, but I managed to pretty much stay cool.

Until Carlos got out of hand.

"Yo, Carlos!" Zo shouted, dribbling the ball at the top of the key. "This one's for you and your weak squad!"

Zo went into a stutter step and then cut to the hoop and went soaring into the air for the layup.

But Carlos must have had enough of Zo's mouth, because he jumped out from under the basket, grabbed Zo in the air, and just threw him down on the asphalt flat out. Zo went skidding across the court.

That's when something inside me snapped. I don't know if it was the heat, or my headache, or just this whole game, but when I saw my boy hit the ground, I charged at Carlos like a rodeo bull.

Before I even knew what I was doing, I knocked Carlos flat on his face.

"Patrick!" I heard Ronnie scream. "What are you doing?"

Carlos jumped up off the ground with a bloody lip and a look in his eye like he was going to kill me.

He came at me, swinging, and caught me in the face with a right hook! He sure was strong. I felt like I'd been hit by a freight train.

I was just about to hit back when I felt a big hand grab the back of my neck, and yank me off the ground.

CHAPTER 5

BUSTED

I peered around to see who the hand that grabbed me belonged to, and looked right up into the face of a very angry Coach Henderson.

"Let go of me, man!" Carlos screamed, trying to break free of Coach Henderson's iron grip. But it was no use; Coach wouldn't let go.

"Cool it, boys," Coach commanded loudly. "Everybody just settle down."

Coach Henderson was the PE teacher at school. And, man, did he look like a PE teacher. He was sporting an old-school jumpsuit and wore a big whistle around his neck. He had gigantic shades, a bushy mustache, and a bald head—if you looked closely, you could see your reflection in it.

"Come on, Coach," I begged. "You're hurting my neck!"

He finally let go of Carlos and me. We were panting like dogs, still trying to stare each other down.

Coach stood between us. The Warriors crowded behind Carlos, and the Bulldogs crowded behind me. We must have looked like we were ready to go to war.

"Does someone want to tell me what's going on here?" Coach asked, looking around at all the kids on the court.

No one said a word. Both teams were looking down at the ground like they'd just dropped some loose change.

"Come on, now," Coach Henderson insisted. "Someone better start talking!"

"I saw the whole thing, Coach!" Zo shouted as he stepped up to Coach Henderson. "It was all Carlos, man! He was mad 'cause I was schoolin' him on the court, so he threw me down and then he clocked Patrick. The boy's crazy! Look at him. Look at those bugged-out eyes. I think he's played too many video games, man."

"Shut your mouth, baby boy." Carlos started to come at Zo, but Coach put his hand on Carlos's chest and pushed him back toward the Warriors.

"That's enough!" Coach ordered as he stood between us. "What's your version of the story?"

"Hey, man, I was just defending myself," Carlos said, waving his hands and his dreds all over the place. He pointed his finger in my face. "*Beanpole* tried to run me down."

"You better stop callin' him Beanpole," Cheryl chimed in from behind me.

"What did you say to me, girl?" Carlos asked, his eyes bulging out at Cheryl.

Suddenly, a loud screeching noise shot through my eardrums. Everyone covered their ears.

Finally, Coach Henderson stopped blowing his whistle.

"That's enough from everyone!" Coach shouted. "This is not the kind of behavior I expect from you. You understand, Patrick?"

Me? What was he talking to me for? I wasn't the one trying to start a fight.

"Now I want you all to go home," Coach went on, trying to look each player in the eye. "If you can't play like good sports, then you shouldn't play at all. Now go on. Get on home."

The Bulldogs and the Warriors started to back away from each other slowly, grumbling with every step. The vibe was most definitely not friendly.

I was still eyeing Carlos and he was trying to flash me his toughest mug. But I knew I'd made my point.

I was saying everything I needed to

say with the look in my eyes. I was silently letting Carlos know that he couldn't scare me, that I'd stand up to him. We didn't need to throw punches. And nothing else needed to be said.

Coach Henderson stayed in the middle of the court to make sure each team left in a different direction.

We were all walking backwards so we could keep staring each other down.

"Yo!" Mile-Wide Elroy shouted. "Carlos would pound that stringbean into the ground any day of the week!"

"You are very wrong, large-nosed short boy," Dikembe answered back. He waved his finger at the Warriors like he was a schoolteacher. "Patrick is very powerful and his moves are extremely dopey!"

"*Dope!*" Zo added quickly, trying to look and sound tough. "That's right—Patrick's got the *dope* moves, boyee! So watch your back, Car-*louse!*"

"Beanpole should not have messed with me!" Carlos screamed.

"Name the day, cuz!" said Zo, turning around again.

"Any day! Any way!" said Carlos.

I couldn't believe my ears. Zo was setting up a fight, and he wasn't even the one who was going to be fighting!

"Chill, Zo," I commanded, as I gave him a little push. "I don't need to throw down to prove who I am."

Before anyone could say another word, Coach screamed, "If I hear one more word, I'm gonna close this court for the whole summer! Now, get on home."

I'm glad that's over with, I thought as I walked slowly off the court with my team.

Patrick Ewing: The Great Warrior

Chapter 6

"Fight? What fight?" I shouted, looking down at Zo in a state of shock.

I had just gotten to the Zone—that's the video arcade a few blocks from Douglass Park where my crew and I like to hang—when Zo walked up and hit me with the news right in front of the snack bar.

"You know what fight," Zo squeaked, dropping some money on the counter for some fries. "You and Carlos, boy. The fight's gonna be on Saturday at Doogy Park. Let's get ready to *r-r-r-u-u-u-u-mble.*"

"Zo, are you crazy?" I said, pounding my hand on the counter. "Is your brain filled up with Nestle's Quik? I told you I wasn't gonna fight that boy."

"Don't worry, Pat." Zo dug me an elbow into my chest. "You'll pound him, baby."

Zo started bumping and grinding, and singing at the top of his lungs. Everyone at the snack bar was looking at him.

"Patrick's gonna pound you, Carlos! Wooo! *Break down!* You hear me? I said Patrick's gonna—*ooomph!*"

I clamped my hand over Zo's monster mouth and moved him over to the closest video game. Everyone at the snack bar was laughing and looking at us like this was a big joke. I had to shut him up.

"What's the matter?"

Zo chirped. "You don't like my singing?"

"It's not your singing—it's your hearing, Zo," I whispered, pushing Zo against the side of the video game. "Look, I don't want to fight him. I don't *need* to fight him. Our thing is over, you understand?"

"No, it's not, Pat," Zo said quietly, "but you can't back out of this fight now. You'll look small, man. And you're gonna make the Bulldogs look like a bunch of chumps!"

"How can I be backing out of a fight I never even backed into?" I growled.

"You the man!" came Fat Craig's voice from behind me.

Fat Craig was standing right next to me with a huge orange grin on his face. He was pounding down fistfuls of Cheez Doodles. I guess I don't have to tell you why we call him "Fat Craig."

"Yo, Pat, thanks for standing up for us, man," Fat Craig went on. "I knew we could count on you. Standing up to Carlos is strong, yo. The Bulldogs gotta make a statement, you know what I'm sayin'?"

"There's not going to be any fight," I told him.

"What are you talking about?" Fat Craig asked. "You're backing down?"

"How can I back down?" I shouted. "I never even said I was going to—!"

Cheryl interrupted me as she found us by the video game.

"Mack Daddy!" she called to me. "Daddy Mack. I knew you weren't gonna let that musclehead push us around."

She and Fat Craig pounded fists.

"Wait a minute," I said. "No one's listening to what I'm saying! I'm not a fighter, I'm a—"

Suddenly I heard a weird shout come from the other side of the arcade. It sounded like some kind of crazy birdcall or something.

We all turned our heads toward the doorway of the Zone. And there was Dikembe.

He was pumping his fist high up in the air, looking me fiercely in the eyes, and hooting this freaky noise at the top of his lungs. It looked like the boy had bugged out completely.

We all ran up to him as fast as we could.

"Dikembe!" I screamed. "Cut it out, man. You'll get us kicked out of here."

Dikembe suddenly stopped hooting, and a huge grin spread across his face. He put his hand on my shoulder.

"Patrick, my brother," Dikembe said, smiling. "This was a war cry from Zaire."

"Yeah, well, you can't go around shouting war cries from Zaire at the Zone," I said.

"Okay," said Dikembe. "Thank you for this tip. But this was a call of respect for you, Patrick. You show great courage by facing Carlos."

Oh, man. Even *Dikembe* wanted me to fight? I couldn't believe it.

"Dikembe," I said, pulling him over by the video game, where we could talk a little more privately. "I'm not going to fight, man."

"Patrick," said Dikembe, gripping my shoulder again. "My ancestors in Zaire were peaceful people. But sometimes we needed great warriors to fight for us; to stand up for us. It is like I said before. Carlos and his friends should be ashamed to call themselves warriors. You will be the true warrior."

"Right on!" Zo shouted. "That's right, Pat. You're our warrior. Our hero. You're standing up for the Bulldogs and protecting Douglass Park from the so-called bad boys of Thompsonville."

"Words, Alonzo!" said Dikembe as he slapped Zo on the back.

"Huh?" Alonzo grunted.

"Uhh . . . " Dikembe hesitated. "Words?"

"Oh, *word*. You mean *word*." Zo smiled.

"Yes, exactly." Dikembe laughed, and slapped Zo on the back even harder. "*Word*, Alonzo," Dikembe shouted, smiling. "And because Patrick is our warrior, I have brought him this from my house."

Dikembe reached carefully into a big

plastic bag and pulled out a beaded necklace with a long white rock at the end.

"What is *that*?" asked Cheryl.

"It is ivory," Dikembe said, as he put the necklace over my head. "This was worn by the warriors of Zaire. And now it is for Patrick."

Dikembe stepped back.

My whole team stood there, looking up at me with these big shiny smiles.

"Yo! Give it up for Patrick Ewing, the Great Warrior!" Zo called.

"*Boo-yaa!*" the Bulldogs cheered.

Suddenly, I had no idea what to do. I didn't want to fight Carlos; I didn't believe in fighting, period. But all this talk about being a great warrior, and standing up for your crew . . . it was starting to make sense. I mean, how could I say no when my crew was asking me to fight *for them?*

I didn't have a choice anymore. I couldn't let the Bulldogs down.

"I'll fight," I said.

"Yeah!" the Bulldogs cheered.

"Okay!" Dikembe announced. "Let's get to work!"

"Who's going to work?" I asked.

"You are," said Dikembe. "A great fighter must train."

CHAPTER 7

GETTING PUMPED

"Hi, Ma!" Zo shouted as we busted through the door to his house. "We'll be in the basement!"

"Okay, sweetheart," came his mother's voice from the kitchen.

Five pairs of feet thundered down the stairs. There was a trunk in one corner of the basement rec room. Zo opened the trunk, grabbed a jump rope, and threw it over to Dikembe, who tossed it to me.

Zo placed his finger on the switch to his boom box and looked to Dikembe for a signal. Cheryl and Fat Craig were doing something with a bunch of empty boxes they had found at the far end of the room.

"Okay, my brother," said Dikembe, as I untwisted the jump rope. "Let us begin the training."

Dikembe looked over at Zo.

"Alonzo," he said. "Let's get gravy."

"Huh?" said Alonzo, his eyebrows drawing together.

"Groovy, Zo!" Cheryl scolded. "He means let's get groovy. Get with the music, man!"

"Oh, right," said Zo, smiling.

"Jump, Patrick! Jump!" Dikembe shouted. "Jump to the music.

Keep it up! One, two, three, four—we're going to do two hundred and fifty of these, so let's go!"

"Yeah, come on, Patrick," said Fat Craig, munching noisily on his Cheez Doodles and sitting in a big cushy chair. "C'mon! let's see some hustle!"

Like that boy had ever jumped rope in his life.

After a half hour of this, it was push-up time. Then it was push-ups with Fat Craig sitting on my back! Then it was sit-ups. Then it was sit-ups with Fat Craig sitting on my legs. That didn't really make the sit-ups any harder, but it did put my legs to sleep.

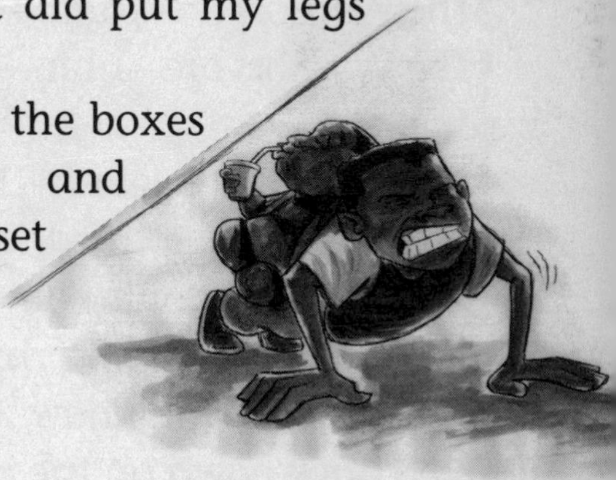

Next I used the boxes Fat Craig and Cheryl had set up as an obstacle course. I ran around them, while throwing punches in the air. I was pumping, and hooking, and jabbing, and the sweat was pouring down my face.

Fat Craig jumped up and started jogging in place, screaming out some rhymes for me to repeat like we were in the army.

"Carlos plays hoops like a little girl . . ."

"Carlos plays hoops like a little girl!" I answered, trying to catch my breath while running and jabbing.

"His face looks like vanilla-fudge swirl!" called Fat Craig.

"His face looks like vanilla-fudge swirl!" I answered, and the others joined in.

"The Warriors are—uhm—a big disaster!"

"The Warriors are—uhm—a big disaster," we answered.

"And we will celebrate by . . . eating pasta?" We all groaned, and Fat Craig pouted. "Well, I don't know! I'm hungry! Somebody else do some rhyming. I can't do it all myself, you know," he said, as he flopped back down on the couch.

After a while, Ronnie showed up. I guess Zo's mom had told him we were hanging downstairs.

"Yo, Ronnie," Fat Craig said, reaching for his Cheez Doodles. "Sing out a good fighting rhyme for Patrick's training."

Ronnie frowned. He didn't look very happy, standing at the top of the basement stairs.

"Come on, Ronnie!" I said, running by him on my little obstacle course. "I'm getting pumped, man."

"You want a fighting rhyme?" said Ronnie. "Here's my fighting rhyme: Patrick always does what's right / That is why he should not fight."

"*Awwwww!*" the Bulldogs groaned. Cheryl waved her arm at Ronnie, and Fat Craig threw a Cheez Doodle at him.

"Come on, scaredy-cat," said Zo. "Stop being such a wimp. Pat's gonna house Carlos."

"Yeah," said Cheryl. "Your attitude is getting on my nerves, Ronnie."

I had to admit, maybe Ronnie was right. What if I couldn't handle Carlos? But I was feeling pumped and ready to go. I didn't want to let the others down. "Look, Ronnie," I said, "I'll handle this my way. You don't have to come and watch if you don't want to. And you don't have to be on the team anymore, either. That's fine with me."

Ronnie looked hurt, but I didn't care.

I didn't want to see Carlos pushing anyone else around. Not on my court.

"I'm feeling strong!" I shouted. "Let's bounce, Bulldogs!" I ran up the stairs, right past Ronnie, and out the front door.

Dikembe ran right after me, then Cheryl. Zo grabbed his boom box and brought it out on the street. Fat Craig tried to keep up, but it's hard to run and eat Cheez Doodles at the same time.

We ran down the street toward Douglass Park, flying past all the trees and the houses. Everything on either side of me was just a big blur as the wind beat against my face and my chest.

The music was pumping and all my teammates were trying to run with me and give me slaps on the back.

But they couldn't keep up with me now, because I was hauling at top speed.

"Yo go, boy!" screamed Cheryl.

"It's all you!" exclaimed Zo.

"You shall be victorious!" said Dikembe.

Fat Craig tried to say something, but all that came out were gasps and crumbs.

As we ran into Douglass Park, it almost seemed like the music got louder. I sprinted up toward the hoop and tapped my hand on the rim.

I came down in the paint and started wildly jumping up and down and pumping my fists.

The Bulldogs were standing around me and cheering. I felt good. I felt strong.

Get ready, Carlos, I thought, *because here I come!*

CHAPTER 8

The rest of the week rolled right by me. Before I knew it, it was already Friday. The day before the fight.

And I'll be straight with you. It's hard to stay pumped for a fight every day. After a while, you start remembering what it really feels like to get popped in the face. It hurts. Especially when it's someone like Carlos who is doing the popping.

And I was starting to get nervous.

I tried to calm myself by shooting some hoops in Doogy Park. I was working on my moves down in the post.

I set my back to the hoop, pounded the rock down twice, faked left, and flipped around and up to my right for the shot.

Swish!

I almost always school my man with that move. I was starting to relax a little.

But then I thought about Carlos again. This wasn't a game of one-on-one.

This was a fistfight. And Carlos was huge. This fight could cause us both a whole lot of pain. But I had to stand up for my crew, and Carlos definitely needed to be taught a lesson, even if things were going to get pretty messy.

Suddenly I heard something coming from behind the trees.

"Stand up and get served, baby boy," said a voice.

I dropped my ball and quickly ran over to the trees.

"Just back on up!" a little voice screamed.

I'd know *that* voice anywhere. Zo was running his mouth again. I peeked through some bushes and saw him and some other boys in a clearing.

It was Mile-Wide Elroy and that nasty,

Frankenstein-looking D-Rock.

I knew that Zo would kill me if I ran in and tried to defend him. It would seem like I didn't think he could handle himself. So I ran around the clearing to get a better look, and be ready in case things turned ugly.

"The Warriors are tired of your trash-talking," said D-Rock. He was towering over Zo.

"Sorry to hear that," Zo said, waving his hand in D-Rock's face. "'Cause I just thought trash was all you boys would understand!"

D-Rock moved in on Zo a little closer.

"Zo, come on. Let's go," came a voice from behind Zo.

For the first time, I noticed that Zo had someone with him. It was his best friend, Keith Van Horn. Keith was a little younger than Zo, and the two of them hung out all the time. Right now, he was standing a few feet behind Zo.

"Not now, Keith," Zo said. "Can't you

see I'm having a talk with dummy number three, here?"

Now, I always knew Zo was fearless, but was he completely nuts? Was he trying to get himself killed?

"You're gonna get beat down so hard," D-Rock was growling. "You and your weak, ugly, sad crew are all gonna get smacked right out of Douglass Park!"

D-Rock got way up in Zo's face. For a split second, I was sure he was going to hit him.

"Zo, come on," Keith begged. He looked as nervous as I felt.

But Zo wasn't backing down.

Instead, he started clowning D-Rock right to his face.

"Oh, poor Carlos," Zo cried, making like he was one of the Warriors crying. "Why'd we let him fight Patrick? We didn't know Carlos was the weakest boy in Thompsonville. I guess that makes us the biggest scrubs in Thompsonville. Mommy! I want my mommy!"

"That's it!" D-Rock screamed.

Thud!

The homeboy popped Zo right in his gut! Zo doubled over in pain.

"Pound that baby boy!" screamed Mile-Wide Elroy.

I jumped out from behind the trees and threw D-Rock off of Zo.

Keith ran into the mix, too. He was trying to hold Mile-Wide Elroy off.

"Get off him!" I screamed, pushing myself between Zo and D-Rock.

"Break it up!" Keith screamed.

Zo was lying on the ground, coughing and holding on to his stomach. "That . . . didn't . . . hurt," he sputtered, and D-Rock started, like he was going to go after Zo again. "Who taught you to fight—your mommy?"

"Y'all *chill!*" I shouted. "Just chill *out!*"

D-Rock seemed to change his mind. He started coming right for *me!* He reached back to smack me.

"Hold up!" shouted Elroy.

D-Rock stopped right in his tracks and pulled up.

We all froze in place, gasping for breath and looking each other over. I wasn't sure what was going to happen next.

"That's Carlos's boy, man," said Elroy. "Carlos is gonna take care of him tomorrow."

He and D-Rock started to back away.

"Have a nice day, Patricia," D-Rock said and flashed me a nasty smile. "'Cause tomorrow you're gonna be lyin' on the asphalt, hurtin' real bad."

He turned to Zo.

"And don't think we forgot about you, baby boy. You're next. See ya! I wouldn't want to be ya!"

And with that, they turned and ran out of the clearing.

"You okay, Zo?"

I knelt down to check on my boy. D-Rock had gotten in one hard punch.

"Are you all right, man?" asked Keith as he tried to help Alonzo up.

"I'm fine!" Zo coughed, pushing us away.

He got up and started to brush himself off. There was dirt all over his face, and some bruises and scratches, too.

I could tell Zo was embarrassed, so he was trying to act like the big man, like he wasn't hurting. But I knew he was.

"I hate those guys, man!" Zo screamed, clenching his fists and pacing around on the grass. "Patrick, you gotta pound Carlos, man. You gotta show 'em we're tougher than they are, man."

"Why were you making fun of them?" asked Keith, trying to brush Zo off again. "You were just making things worse."

"Shut up, Keith!" Zo snapped, pushing his friend away again. "I *thought* you were my boy. You were supposed to watch my back, man!" he whined. "How come you didn't jump in?"

"I *did* watch your back," Keith insisted. "I just won't fight."

"Why not?" I asked.

"'Cause he doesn't believe in fighting," said Zo sarcastically.

"I can respect that," I said, trying to give props to Keith.

"Oh yeah?" Zo squeaked. "Well, when two kids try to pound my face in the dirt, I'm gonna beat 'em down!" He slammed his fist into his hand.

"But you'll never beat them," I said.

"I know, Patrick! That's why *you* gotta fight! Let them know they messed with the wrong wrecking crew. Take 'em to class!"

Then the weirdest thing happened. Zo's face kind of changed. He didn't look so angry all of a sudden. I know Zo wouldn't admit it, but he started to look kind of sad.

"You think I like being this small?" Zo asked, looking me in the eye. "I hate it. People callin' me baby boy and roughin' me up as much as they want.

"Look at what they did to me, Patrick. Are you gonna let them get away with that? You gotta stand up for me, man. If you're really my ace, you'll end this thing tomorrow."

I took a good look at Zo. A small tear ran

down his face. He had dirt in his hair and all over his clothes. He looked like a mess.

If I hadn't stepped in, who knows how out of hand things could've gotten?

Zo was right. This whole thing had to end. If Carlos and his Warriors thought they could mess with the Bulldogs whenever they wanted, they were crazy.

Nobody roughs up my boy! Nobody roughs up my team!

It was time to send those chumps back where they came from.

"I'll end it," I said, clasping my hand with Zo's. "Tomorrow afternoon, I'm gonna end this thing for good."

SHOWDOWN

CHAPTER 9

The sun was beating down on me even harder than it had the week before. Saturday had arrived, and Douglass Park was boiling.

The time had come for the big showdown.

When I walked onto the court, I could see all my teammates were there already. Even Ronnie had showed up for the fight. That meant a lot to me . . . even if he *was* standing about ten feet away from everybody else.

The rest of my team had already started hollering and talking trash to the Warriors. Let me tell you, the scene was ugly. Dikembe was waving his finger again. Zo was screaming so loud, the veins were popping out of his neck. Cheryl was sliding her head right and left so much, I thought it was going to slide right off. And, of course, Fat Craig was rooting her on.

The Warriors were screaming right back at them from the opposite side of the court. D-Rock and Mile-Wide Elroy looked like two ugly dogs who couldn't stop barking.

The two teams looked ready to brawl, but they were still leaving some room between them at center court for Carlos and me to throw down.

Carlos danced around in center court like he was the heavyweight champion of the world, or something.

Just stay cool, Pat, I told myself, as I walked toward them. *You can take him. Just be strong.*

Carlos did a double take as he saw me coming onto the court. He stopped dancing around and gawked at me.

"You wouldn't understand," I said as I

made my way to center court, and got eye to eye with Carlos.

"Nice necklace, Patricia. Did you borrow it from your sister?" Carlos blurted, practically spitting in my face as I walked up to him. I was wearing the ivory necklace Dikembe had given me.

I wiped my face with my hand and glared into his eyes.

"He is wearing the mark of a great warrior," Dikembe snarled. "Something you definitely would not understand."

"That's right," Zo agreed, jumping out a little from the group.

"Oh, a 'great warrior,' huh?" Carlos scoffed, looking me up and down. "The leader of the *chumps.*"

"No, that would be *you!*" Cheryl yelled. "Patrick! Clean the court with his fat Brillo head!"

"Yeah, Pat," Fat Craig cheered. "Smack this weak crew right out of Doogy Park, boy."

"Yeah!" Zo screamed. "Sock him, Pat! Right now! One punch, baby."

"Come on, Carlos," D-Rock yelled. "Let's see the Beanpole out cold on the asphalt!"

"Make him beg for mercy!" Mile-Wide Elroy called.

The Warriors were out for blood.

I could feel the tension building as Carlos and I stared our hardest stares and clenched our fists for combat. It was just a question of who was going to throw the first punch.

"I've been waiting for this all week," said Carlos, pounding his fist into his other hand. "You shouldn't have pushed me down, Patricia. 'Cause now you're gonna have to pay."

"You just gotta be the baddest boy on the block, don't you?" I asked, looking Carlos up and down with pity. "Even if a kid half your size messes with you, you gotta throw him down on the court. Makes you feel real large, huh? Keeps you feelin' like a big man?"

Carlos's face turned red; I thought he might explode all over me.

"You must be pretty desperate for some respect, big guy," I continued.

"That's it, boy!" Carlos hollered in a rage. "It's on." Carlos was grinding his teeth. "I'm gonna make your mama sorry she let you out. Let's do this!"

He ripped off his jersey like a crazy man and threw it down on the court. I guess he thought a bunch of flexing was going to intimidate me.

"Let's go, Patricia!" he yelled, as he started throwing jabs in the air and moving in and out. "Carlos *is* the biggest man on the block! Time to show! Time to prove!"

I put up my fists, and Carlos and I circled each other.

Keep your guard up, Ewing, I said to myself. *No fear.*

The look in Carlos's eyes told me he wasn't just looking for a few punches. He was looking to do some serious damage. Carlos had something to prove.

His crew was hooting and hollering.

"Beat him down, boy!" D-Rock screamed.

"You go! Take care of business!"

"Come on, Pat!" Cheryl screamed. "Bust him up! Take out the trash!"

Carlos was wearing a wicked smile.

"Come on," he whispered, grinning at me. He pointed at his chin. "Right there, Patricia. I dare you. Just one punch, boy. Then they're all gonna watch you get the beating of your life."

I pulled my fist back.

"Pound him, Pat!" Zo screamed from behind me.

Suddenly, D-Rock started yelling over at Zo from the other side of the court.

"Don't worry, Mighty Mouth!" D-Rock taunted from behind Carlos. "You'll get your turn. You're next, baby boy."

"Anyone who touches Alonzo will have to answer to me," Dikembe shouted.

"Oh yeah?" screamed Mile-Wide Elroy. "Well, then, we'll just have to take care of you after the baby boy, Shaka Zulu!"

The Bulldogs and the Warriors all

started screaming at each other. I could hardly hear myself think.

Suddenly, smack in the middle of all that yapping, I just looked at Carlos grinning at me, daring me to hit him. I listened to the two teams, barking at each other like dogs, talking about how they were all going to beat each other up.

And I realized what I had to do.

Slowly, I dropped my fist to my side, and backed off.

Both teams went completely silent.

Everyone was staring at me just standing there. Everyone looked confused.

"Wassup?" asked Carlos, moving slowly toward me, and pounding his chest. "What are you waiting for, boy?"

I just stood still and didn't move a muscle.

"Yeah, Pat," said Zo. "What are you doing, man?"

I looked Carlos in the eye.

"I'm not gonna fight you," I said.

WALKING AWAY

CHAPTER 10

"What are you talkin' about, boy?" Carlos asked, moving up on me.

"What's the deal, Pat?" asked a very confused Cheryl from behind me.

"I'm not gonna fight you, Carlos," I repeated.

"You're not gonna fight me?" he asked cautiously, looking pretty suspicious.

"That's what I said," I replied.

"A'right," Carlos mumbled, still trying to stare me down. "Well, then, what do you think of this?"

Carlos suddenly hauled off and clocked me right in my face.

Whack!

The punch rocked me,

whipping my head to the side. I almost lost my balance. I felt my fist clench up again. Man, did I want to hit him right back.

"Come on, punk!" Carlos screamed, pounding his hands on his chest. "What do you think about that, Patricia? What you gonna do now?"

The Warriors started shouting again, trying to get this party started. The Bulldogs were shouting too. They wanted me to hit back.

But somehow, I managed to unclench my fist.

"Nothing," I said. "I'm just not gonna do anything."

I felt a little dizzy; I couldn't believe I was really doing this. For all I knew, Carlos might just start whaling on me.

And my team probably thought I was chickening out.

But this was how it had to be. And I couldn't turn back.

I had come to Douglass Park to end this thing with Carlos and the Warriors, not to start some big feud between our two teams that would never end. The fighting had to stop.

I remembered what Zo had looked like after D-Rock had hit him. I couldn't let something like that happen again. No way.

"You're an even bigger chicken than I thought, Patricia!" Carlos shouted. "Yo, fellas, Beanpole's chickening out!"

His whole crew started laughing.

"I knew he couldn't fight," screamed D-Rock.

"Listen to that, man," Zo whined from behind me. "Smack him, Pat! What are you doing?"

I knew Zo thought I was letting him down, but I had to be strong.

"What's your problem, Beanpole?"

Carlos taunted. "You thinkin' about how hard you're gonna get beat?"

Carlos poked me in the chest. He yanked on my ivory necklace. He was doing anything he could think of to get a rise out of me.

He gave me a little slap on the face.

"Come on, boy," he taunted, and *slap! "Does that hurt*?" he asked, *slap!*

I was trying to stay cool, but I wanted to pound him so bad. If he gave me one more of those little slaps, I swear I was going to rip his head off.

My teammates were inching toward us at every little slap. Dikembe and Zo were creeping up on us, and even Cheryl looked like she was going to start whaling on somebody. If I wasn't going to start hitting Carlos, then they were.

Carlos was coming at me with another little slap. But it was the last one I was going to take.

Just as his hand was about to hit my

face, I reached up and grabbed his wrist with all my strength.

The Bulldogs stopped cold in their tracks.

The Warriors let out a gasp, and fell completely silent.

I held Carlos's arm for a minute, and just looked at him. I could feel his pulse racing as I held firm to his wrist. He could barely move his arm.

And for the first time, Carlos stopped talking. He wasn't showing off for anybody. He didn't know what to do.

"Carlos," I said, still holding his arm tightly, and squeezing it as hard as I could. "If I fight you, where's it gonna end, man? The Bulldogs come to Douglass Park to play basketball, not to fight. Give me a ball, and I'll school you. All fighting does is start more fighting. Forget it, man. It's over."

I threw down his wrist, turned around, and started walking away.

No one said a word. Carlos stood at center court, with his mouth hanging open.

I wasn't even sure if my team was going to follow me. I was crossing my fingers, hoping they would understand why I did what I did. I needed them to walk with me. I wanted us to walk away as a team.

But no one moved or spoke at all. I think they were all in shock from the way I'd just shut down Carlos. They didn't know what to do.

I turned around and called to my squad.

"Come on, y'all," I said. "We've wasted enough time with this crew."

Still no one moved, and for a second, I was sure that my team had given up on me. Then Dikembe began slowly backing away from the Warriors.

Dikembe flashed Carlos one last nasty look and then he turned to walk with me.

Cheryl looked at Carlos, who was still just standing there like a fool. She looked him over from top to bottom and then just let out a little grunt like she was saying, "You ain't nothin'."

"Come on, Fat Craig," she said as she turned around and walked toward me and Dikembe. He followed her.

That left only Zo, and he was definitely crazy enough to try to take on all of the Warriors single-handed. He was frowning at Carlos, trying to look tough.

"Come on, Zo," I called to him. "Don't sweat that dude. He ain't worth it."

Zo looked over at the Bulldogs, and then back at the Warriors. He opened his mouth, and I let out a groan, imagining what he was going to say.

"See ya," he said to Carlos. "I wouldn't want to be ya."

Zo turned and walked toward us.

Then the Bulldogs all started to walk off the court as a team.

I headed toward Ronnie, who'd been standing as far away as he could from the whole scene. For the first time in a week, instead of looking sour and scared, he looked happy.

He came up to me and slapped his hand on my shoulder.

"That was smooth, my friend," Ronnie said as he gave me an elbow to my chest. "That was real smooth."

I smiled at him. "You were right," I said.

He shrugged and gave me a goofy smile. "I know."

"Friends, right?" I said, pounding fists with him.

"Best friends," he said with a smile. "You stood up for all of us, man."

I turned around with my teammates and we all headed off the court.

"Hey!" Carlos hollered from behind us. "You can't just walk away! Come back here! Hey!"

Carlos was sounding pretty desperate. We just ignored him as we marched out of Douglass Park.

"Y'all come back here right now!" Carlos called. "I said come back here!"

He was practically begging. And he sounded so small.

"Yo, Carlos, let's go get them, man!" D-Rock shouted.

"*Shut up!*" he screamed back at D-Rock. "You don't tell me what to do, boy. Nobody tells me what to do! 'Cause I'm Carlos, man! I'm Carlos!"

Suddenly, a loud whistle blew on the court.

"That will be quite enough, Gentlemen!"

We all stopped at the fence and looked back at center court.

"Yo, it's Coach Henderson again," said Fat Craig with a big smile on his face.

Coach had run onto the court and he was holding Carlos and D-Rock by the neck.

"What did I tell you boys about fighting on this court?" Coach Henderson shouted. "That's it! You're all coming with me, and we're going to see what your parents have to say about all this fighting."

"Get off of me, man!" screamed Carlos, trying to break free of Coach's grip. "Get off of meeeee. . . ."

Coach escorted the Warriors out of Douglass Park.

My friends and I couldn't help laughing; the Warriors looked ridiculous as Coach Henderson made them line up and march off the court like a bunch of kindergartners.

And that was the last we ever saw of bad boy Carlos and his ugly crew.

LEARNING A LESSON

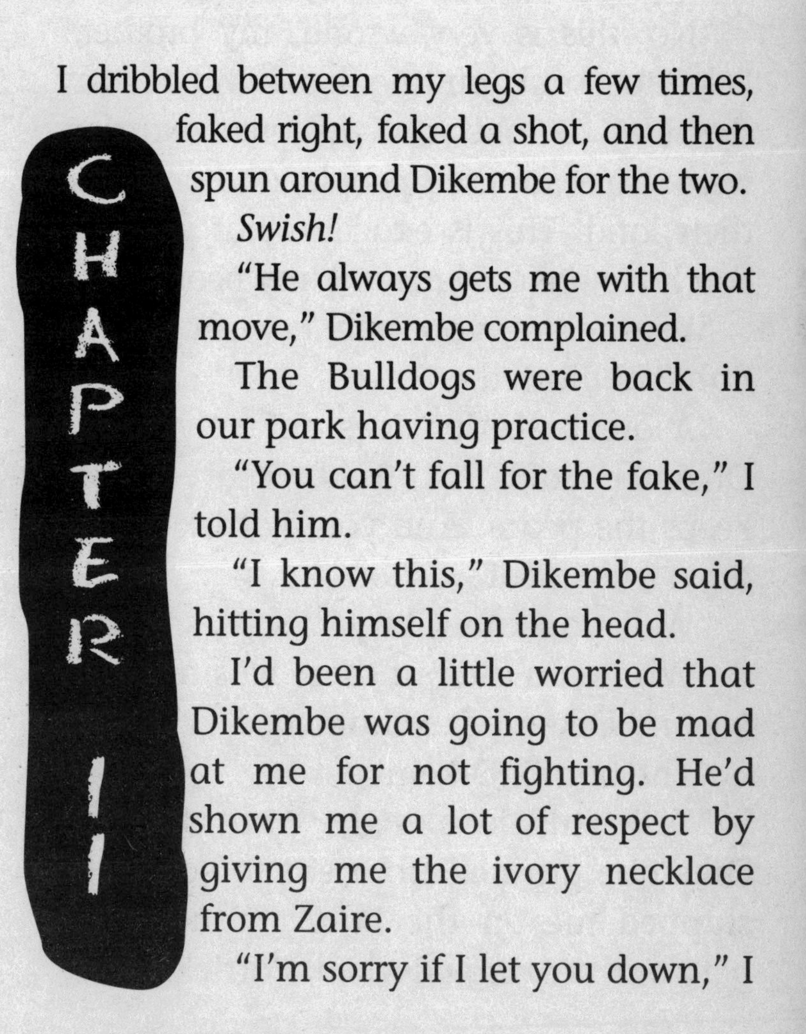

I dribbled between my legs a few times, faked right, faked a shot, and then spun around Dikembe for the two.

Swish!

"He always gets me with that move," Dikembe complained.

The Bulldogs were back in our park having practice.

"You can't fall for the fake," I told him.

"I know this," Dikembe said, hitting himself on the head.

I'd been a little worried that Dikembe was going to be mad at me for not fighting. He'd shown me a lot of respect by giving me the ivory necklace from Zaire.

"I'm sorry if I let you down," I

said to Dikembe, holding on to the ball.

"But why are you sorry?" Dikembe asked.

"Because I didn't fight like you wanted me to," I said. "I wasn't a great warrior."

"No, this is very wrong, my brother," Dikembe said, putting his hand on my shoulder. "I told you, the great warriors were strong for their people, and protected their land. This is exactly what you did. You have honored me and my people!"

"You mean you *didn't* want me to fight?" I blurted.

"A great warrior does not only fight," Dikembe said. "A truly great warrior keeps the peace. And you, Patrick Ewing, are a truly great warrior."

"Well, you know, I try," I said, smiling.

"What you did out there was truly the *boom!*" Dikembe exclaimed.

"The bomb, Dikembe."

"Yes! This is exactly what I said!" Dikembe grinned from ear to ear as he slapped me on the back. "You should get your hearing checked, Patrick."

"Patrick is the man!" Zo shouted, grabbing the ball and firing a jumper right through the net.

Zo had been yapping about me all day. The boy could not close his mouth.

"Yo, Ronnie," Zo called. "*Is* Patrick or is Patrick *not* the man?"

"He's the man," said Ronnie, smiling.

"I mean, did you see the way he took on Carlos yesterday?" Zo threw out his arm like he was holding Carlos's wrist. "He was like, Yo—there ain't gonna be no fight. It's over!"

Zo went up for the layup and flipped the ball in the hoop.

"It was beautiful, man."

Zo passed the ball over to Fat Craig, who went straight up for the shot.

Swish!

Zo grabbed the ball and started dribbling again.

"Yo, Keith," he said. Zo's friend Keith was hanging with us on the sidelines. "Is Patrick or is Patrick not the man?"

"He's the man, Zo," said Keith, giving me a thumbs-up. I flashed him a smile.

"Carlos was beggin' for a fight," Zo went on, "and Pat just wouldn't give it to him. He just walked away. That was so dope! That was *off the hook*, baby."

I got a real kick out of hearing Zo change his tune from the day before.

All he wanted to do all week was trade punches with Carlos and his crew, and now he was totally hyped on walking away.

But just because Zo had learned how to walk away from a scrap, that didn't mean he'd learned how to shut his big mouth.

"Yo, Carlos ain't nothin', boy," Zo said, dribbling the ball between his legs. "He ain't nothin'. Pat proved it yesterday, right?"

"Alonzo!" Dikembe shouted, taking the ball away from Zo and holding on to it. "Why are you never silent? You are always talking."

"Huh?" Zo grunted. "What's he talking about?"

"I think he's just trying to say, maybe if

you didn't talk so much trash, you wouldn't get into so much trouble," I explained.

"Yes," said Dikembe. "This is exactly what I mean."

"I know that's right," Cheryl said, and Fat Craig chimed in with an "Mmm-hmm."

Zo just stared at all of us in disbelief. Then he started chuckling.

"You so crazy, Dikembe," he laughed. He looked around at the rest of us. "Is he crazy or what?"

Nobody answered. We all just looked at Zo.

"Y'all are crazy!" Zo insisted. "If I stop talkin' . . . how's anyone gonna know what I'm *thinkin'*? Stop trippin', Dikembe."

Dikembe rolled his eyes and shook his head. Cheryl rolled her eyes, too. I guess we all did.

Zo grabbed the ball back and started hoisting up shots again.

"If I stopped talkin'," he said to himself, as he handled the ball, "how's anyone gonna know I'm the Mack Daddy of hoops? How's anyone gonna know I got the skills to pay the bills? I got soul and I roll to the hole, don't snooze or doze, 'cause everybody knows I be rippin' up shows . . ."

I smiled.

I guess Zo will have to learn one lesson at a time.

PATRICK'S POINTERS #2—DRIBBLING

Have you got total control when you dribble . . . like the ball's glued to your hands? Well, here's how to develop those sticky fingers:

TIP #1—RHYTHM

Really good dribblers look almost like they're dancing. Their entire body moves to the pounding rhythm of the ball. If you're having trouble finding this rhythm, turn on the radio and dribble-dance to the beat!

TIP #2—KEEP IT LOW

A high-bouncing dribble is easy to steal. Stay crouched and keep the ball at knee height. If defenders want to steal it from you, they know they'll have to get down and dirty!

TIP #3—THE SHIELD

Remember: Your body is your shield. Always keep part of your body—shoulder, back, or arm—between the ball and your defender. Even the best defenders can't get through a body shield.